A BEAUTIFUL STORY
JESUS & ST. NICK

WRITTEN BY
Sarah French

ILLUSTRATED BY
Robert Sauber

First published in 2023

BNC
B O O K S

Charlotte, NC

Text © 2023 Sarah French
Illustrations © 2023 Robert Sauber

Library of Congress Control Number: 2022921603

ISBN 979-8-9865344-0-4 (Hardback)
979-8-9865344-1-1 (Paperback)

www.SarahSFrench.com

To my children,
I love seeing Christmas through your eyes.
You inspired me to write this book so you would always
know the history behind our Christmas traditions.

To my grandmother,
Thank you for always making Christmas such a magical holiday.
One can only hope to be as loving and giving as you.

This is dedicated to my darling adventurous
equine devoted daughter.

There is a deeply spiritual loveliness in her and

a gift of beautiful humanity whenever you talk to her.

On Christmas Eve, Blair and CJ were frosting the cookies they'd baked for Santa.

"Time for bed," Mommy said.

Blair carefully carried the cookies and milk to the fireplace. But when she set them down, she noticed one of the cookies she decorated was missing!

"Where's my cookie?" she asked. "CJ, where are you?"

CJ had disappeared. Vanished. Vamoosed.

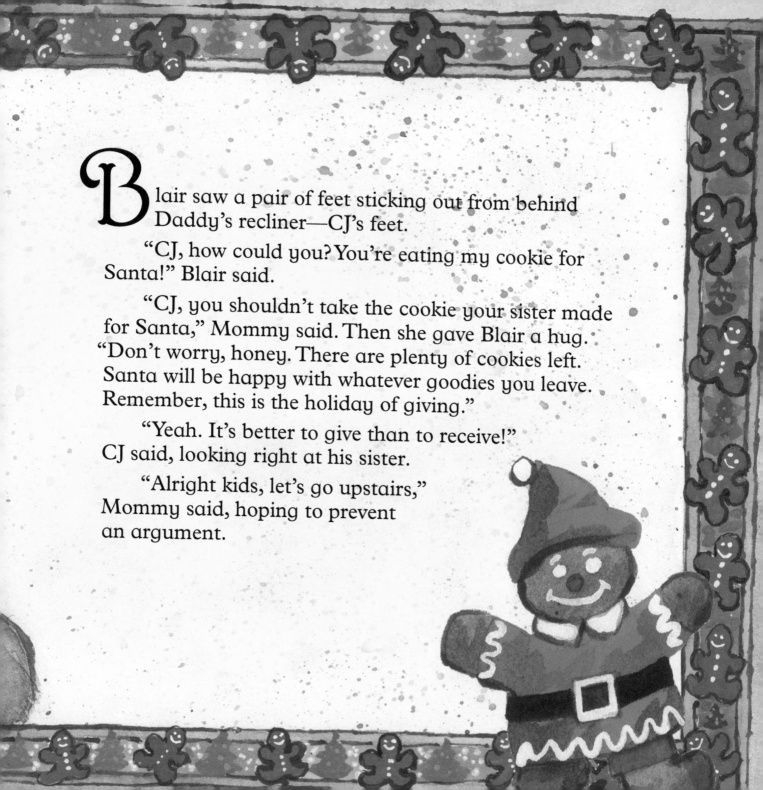

B lair saw a pair of feet sticking out from behind Daddy's recliner—CJ's feet.

"CJ, how could you? You're eating my cookie for Santa!" Blair said.

"CJ, you shouldn't take the cookie your sister made for Santa," Mommy said. Then she gave Blair a hug. "Don't worry, honey. There are plenty of cookies left. Santa will be happy with whatever goodies you leave. Remember, this is the holiday of giving."

"Yeah. It's better to give than to receive!" CJ said, looking right at his sister.

"Alright kids, let's go upstairs," Mommy said, hoping to prevent an argument.

"Where's Mr. Owl?" CJ asked. He always snuggled with Mr. Owl to listen to the bedtime story.

"Buddy has him!" Blair exclaimed. "I'll get him back!"

"That's okay," CJ said. "Mr. Owl is my favorite, but it's Christmas so I'll share with Buddy. It's my gift to him."

Blair bent down next to their dog and whispered, "I'm coming to get him as soon as CJ falls asleep. You can't keep that owl all night. You're sure to chew off an eye or an ear."

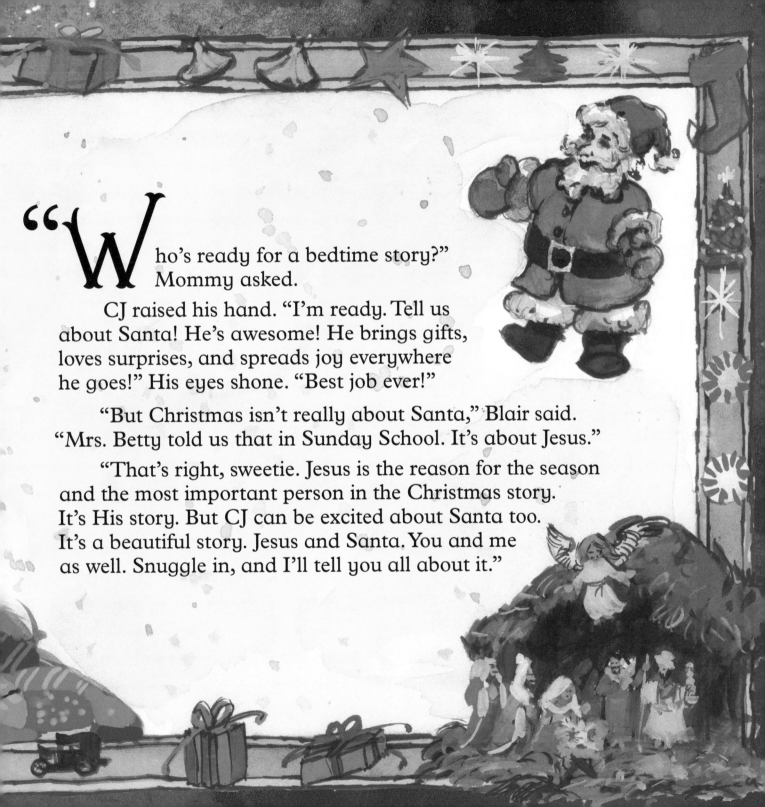

"Who's ready for a bedtime story?" Mommy asked.

CJ raised his hand. "I'm ready. Tell us about Santa! He's awesome! He brings gifts, loves surprises, and spreads joy everywhere he goes!" His eyes shone. "Best job ever!"

"But Christmas isn't really about Santa," Blair said. "Mrs. Betty told us that in Sunday School. It's about Jesus."

"That's right, sweetie. Jesus is the reason for the season and the most important person in the Christmas story. It's His story. But CJ can be excited about Santa too. It's a beautiful story. Jesus and Santa. You and me as well. Snuggle in, and I'll tell you all about it."

For to us a child is born, to us a son is given;
and the government shall be upon his shoulder,
and his name shall be called Wonderful Counselor,
Mighty God, Everlasting Father, Prince of Peace.
ISAIAH 9:6

Therefore the Lord himself will give you a sign.
Behold, the virgin shall conceive and bear a son,
and shall call his name Immanuel.
ISAIAH 7:14

"These scriptures were written by Isaiah more than 700 years before Jesus' birthday," Mommy explained. "Isaiah was a prophet who talked about the Prince of Peace who would come. Immanuel means 'God is with us.' He was talking about Jesus."

Mommy flipped some pages in her Bible. "When Jesus was born, an angel appeared to the shepherds and said, 'This will be a sign for you: you will find a baby wrapped in swaddling cloths and lying in a manger.' The shepherds hurried to Bethlehem, and they found baby Jesus lying in a manger just as the angel had said. His mother, Mary, and His earthly father, Joseph, were with Him."

"But what about Santa and all the gifts he gives away?" CJ asked. "I thought you said this was his story too."

Blair interrupted her brother. "Mommy is telling us about the best gift. Jesus! He came down from Heaven to save all of us. He was a gift from God to the world."

"That's right," Mommy said. "John 3:16 says, 'For God so loved the world, that He gave His only Son, that whoever believes in Him should not perish but have eternal life.' Isn't that incredible?"

CJ took a deep breath. "God gave a special gift when He gave Jesus."

"He is the greatest gift," Mommy added.

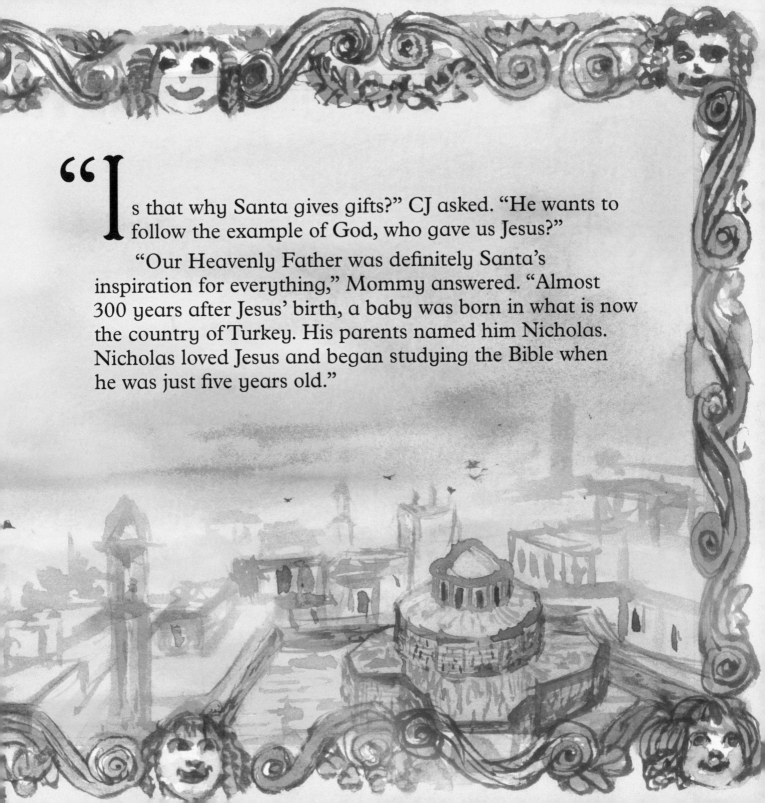

"Is that why Santa gives gifts?" CJ asked. "He wants to follow the example of God, who gave us Jesus?"

"Our Heavenly Father was definitely Santa's inspiration for everything," Mommy answered. "Almost 300 years after Jesus' birth, a baby was born in what is now the country of Turkey. His parents named him Nicholas. Nicholas loved Jesus and began studying the Bible when he was just five years old."

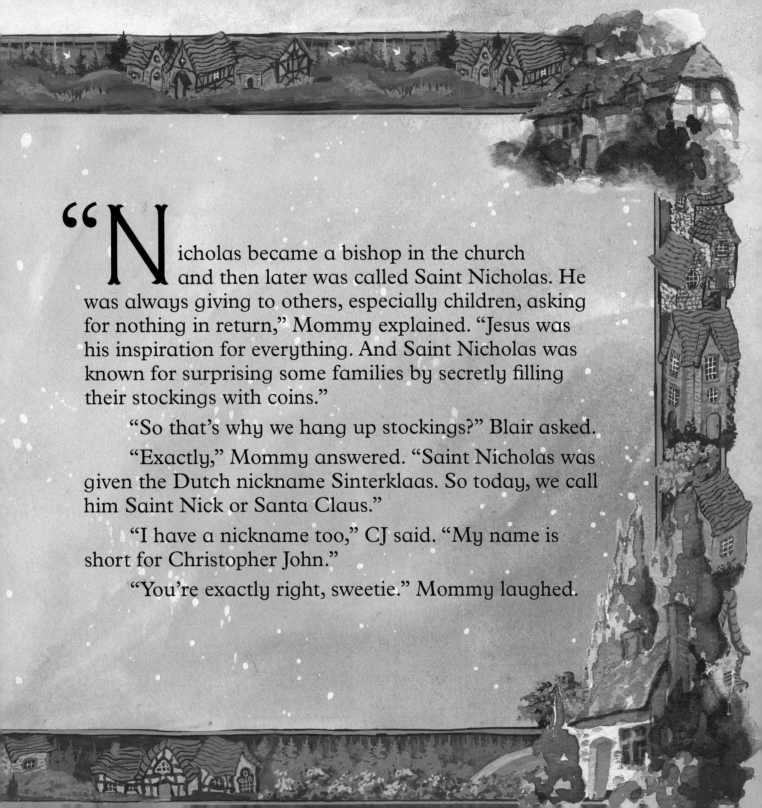

"Nicholas became a bishop in the church and then later was called Saint Nicholas. He was always giving to others, especially children, asking for nothing in return," Mommy explained. "Jesus was his inspiration for everything. And Saint Nicholas was known for surprising some families by secretly filling their stockings with coins."

"So that's why we hang up stockings?" Blair asked.

"Exactly," Mommy answered. "Saint Nicholas was given the Dutch nickname Sinterklaas. So today, we call him Saint Nick or Santa Claus."

"I have a nickname too," CJ said. "My name is short for Christopher John."

"You're exactly right, sweetie." Mommy laughed.

"Saint Nick once said, 'The giver of every good and perfect gift has called upon us to mimic God's giving, by grace, through faith, and this is not of ourselves.' God tells us in the Bible, 'It is more blessed to give than receive' and 'God loves a person who gives cheerfully.' Saint Nick used his money to help others. And today, people continue to do the same."

"I see," Blair said. "Santa wanted to give to others like the Bible says because he was a follower of Jesus."

"And Jesus was the best gift of all," CJ added.

"I think you kids got it." Mommy smiled. "And we're a part of the story too. We can give to others and be like Santa. And we can be ambassadors for Jesus just like Saint Nick."

"Now time for sleep. Christmas morning will be here before you know it."

Mommy kissed them goodnight, and they closed their eyes.

Blair heard something. *Maybe the jingle of a bell*, she thought.

Was it Santa?

Blair looked over, and her brother was already fast asleep. Buddy was too, sleeping right next to Mr. Owl. She decided to let this one slide. And in the spirit of giving, Blair took her favorite stuffed animal, Pink Teddy, and tucked him in with CJ.

Blair closed her eyes and prayed, "Thank you, God, for giving us the gift of Jesus, your Son, who came into the world to save us. Help us all be ambassadors for you, like St. Nick, and help us remember it is more important to give than to receive. In Jesus' name we pray. Amen."

ABOUT THE AUTHOR

Sarah French is a four-time Emmy Award-winning journalist. She is a broadcast news anchor for the NBC affiliate in Charlotte, North Carolina. Sarah was inspired to write this book for her children to explain the story of Christmas with Jesus and Saint Nick as one cohesive story. The Christmas season is Sarah's favorite time of year, and she's overjoyed to share this book with you. Sarah grew up in Arkansas and has a Master of Journalism degree from the University of Missouri School of Journalism.

Sarah loves living in the Carolinas with her husband and two children, Blair and CJ. They have two dogs, Buddy and Teddy. Sarah serves in the children's ministry of her church in Charlotte.

For more information, visit www.SarahSFrench.com.

About the Illustrator

Artist Robert Sauber developed a passion for art from an early age, illustrating ads for local stores. He created children's filmstrips for Gallaudet University, Washington, DC, teaching deaf kids how to read. Robert received his B.A. from the Art Center College of Design in Los Angeles, where he was the first student in his class to be honored to have a painting in the Art Center gallery. In New York City, he developed book covers, magazine stories, and children's books for companies such as Random House and Simon & Schuster.

Storytelling in paintings has always been his passion, to bring out a painted note of humanity that is in all of us, especially in nature and landscapes, something that reflects you, and you can say, "I want to be there!" www.RobertSauber.com

Printed in the USA
CPSIA information can be obtained
at www.ICGtesting.com
LVHW061713190923
758631LV00016B/238